Elle
the Thumbelina
Fairy

Special thanks to Rachel Elliot

ISBN 978-1-338-05495-8

10 9 8 7 6 5 4 3 2 1   17 18 19 20 21

Printed in the U.S.A.   40
First edition, March 2017

Elle
the Thumbelina
Fairy

by Daisy Meadows

SCHOLASTIC INC.

The Fairyland Palace

Fairyland Library

The Three Bears' Cottage

Island

Thumbelina's Cottage

Storybook World

Rapunzel's Tower

Red Riding Hood's Grandmother's House

Red Riding Hood Woods

Jack Frost's
Ice Castle

Storytelling Festival Site

Wetherbury Village

Story Barge

Riverbank

The fairies want stories to stay just the same.
But I've planned a funny and mischievous game.
I'll change all their tales without further ado,
By adding some tricks and a goblin or two!

The four magic stories will soon be improved
When everything that's nice and sweet is removed.
Their dull happy endings are ruined and lost,
For no one's as smart as handsome Jack Frost!

Contents

The Storytelling Festival

Rachel Walker skipped along the riverside path, enjoying the warmth of the sun and the scent of flowers in the air. Her best friend, Kirsty Tate, did a cartwheel beside her and laughed. It was always exciting to spend a weekend together, but this weekend was going to be extra special. They were going to the Wetherbury Storytelling Festival, and they could hardly wait.

"Hurry up, Mom!" called Kirsty, looking back down the path. "It's almost time!"

Their favorite author, Alana Yarn, was going to be sharing her best storytelling tips, and the girls were really looking forward to seeing her.

"Don't worry, we won't be late," said Mrs. Tate with a smile. "Look, the festival tents are just up ahead. Besides, my cartwheeling days are over, Kirsty."

"I'm never going to stop doing cartwheels, even when I'm grown up," said Kirsty.

She grinned at Rachel.

They reached the bright festival tents, which were decorated with bunting and huge book pages.

"They look like they come from a giant's book," said Rachel in delight.

"I do miss getting lost in storybook worlds," said Mrs. Tate. "The books I loved best as a child were filled with imaginary things like magic and fairies."

Kirsty and Rachel exchanged a smile. They knew that fairies were real, not imaginary! In fact, they had lots of fairy friends, but they were the only two people who knew about it.

"Oh, look!" Kirsty exclaimed.

She pointed to where a boat was moored by the riverbank. There was a sign on the path beside it that said, *Story Barge*, and the boat itself was piled high with books. A man was standing on the barge, smiling at them.

"Are you here to see Alana Yarn?" he called.

The girls nodded, and Mrs. Tate smiled.

"Have fun, both of you," she said. "I'll see you later."

She hugged them good-bye and then they skipped over to the Story Barge.

"Welcome to the Storytelling Festival," the man said. "Alana Yarn is about to start. Have a seat over there on the lawn. She won't be long!" Rachel and Kirsty hurried over to where a large group of children was sitting on cushions. They were in a circle around a bench that was shaped like a book. There weren't very many empty cushions left, but the girls found two next to each other and sat down.

"I feel like I might burst, I'm so excited!" said Rachel.

"Me too," Kirsty replied. "I can't believe that Alana Yarn is actually going to be here!"

They had read all of Alana Yarn's books, and had even waited in a long line at the bookstore when a new one came out. The other children in the group looked thrilled, too.

"She's here!" someone exclaimed.

Heads bobbed and necks craned as everyone tried to see the famous author. Rachel and Kirsty glimpsed a mane of curly black hair. Then Alana Yarn took her seat on the book-shaped bench and smiled at her audience. She had a wide, warm smile and sparkling blue eyes with thick, black lashes.

"Welcome to the

Wetherbury Storytelling Festival," said
Alana. "I hope you're as excited as I am
about this weekend. I want you all to be
inspired to tell stories yourselves, and to
let your imaginations soar. At the end
of the weekend, you will all have the
chance to tell a story of your own,
using the new skills you've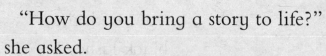
learned. Are there
any questions?"

Rachel felt as
if she was bubbling
over with questions!
She raised her
hand, and Alana
nodded at her.

"How do you bring a story to life?"
she asked.

"Sometimes the simplest way is the

best," Alana replied. "Right now we're going to begin by reading aloud."

There was a stack of books beside her, which she handed around to the crowd of children.

"Make sure everyone gets a copy," she said.

When Rachel and Kirsty got their copies, Kirsty gave a little squeak of happiness. The book they were going to read was *Thumbelina*—one of her favorite stories.

A Magical Library

"Follow along with the story in your own book," said Alana, opening her copy and starting to read aloud. "Once upon a time, there was a woman who longed for children but had none. At last, she went to visit a fairy and said..."

Rachel and Kirsty were swept up in the story. Alana had a lovely reading voice, and the girls felt as if they could almost see tiny Thumbelina in her happy home, sleeping in her little walnut-shell bed.

"One night, when Thumbelina was asleep under her rose-petal quilt, a

goblin crept in through the window," Alana read. "The goblin thought that Thumbelina would make a pretty wife for him, so he scooped her up from her walnut-shell bed and jumped out of the window into the garden."

Kirsty and Rachel glanced at each other.

"That isn't how the story is supposed to go," Kirsty whispered.

"But that's what it says in the book," Rachel replied in a low voice. "Look!"

Kirsty frowned and put up her hand. Alana stopped reading.

"Is everything all right?" she asked in a kind voice.

"I'm sorry to interrupt," said Kirsty, "but I think these books have a mistake in them. Thumbelina is supposed to be carried away by a toad, not a goblin."

"Oh!" said Alana, looking surprised. "I'm certain that it's a goblin. After all, that's what the book says."

All the other children in the circle shot puzzled glances at Kirsty. They obviously thought that she was wrong, too.

"She's right," said Rachel in a loud voice.

But the other children were shaking their heads and making shushing noises. Alana started reading the story again, and Kirsty looked at Rachel with a worried expression.

"Something's wrong," she whispered. "I know this story very well and there definitely aren't any goblins in it!"

Just then, the empty cushion beside

Rachel gave a little quiver. Kirsty and Rachel stared at it in astonishment. The other children were looking at Alana, so no one else noticed as the cushion hopped, shook, and jumped. Then, surrounded by a sprinkle of pale blue fairy dust, a beautiful fairy fluttered out from under the cushion.

"Hello!" she said in an excited whisper. "I'm Elle the Thumbelina Fairy, and I've come to take you both to Fairyland!"

Rachel and Kirsty were so surprised that they stared at Elle in silence for a moment. She was as tiny as Thumbelina herself, with long, wavy hair and an exquisite pale blue dress. Her wings were light pink with curled tips, and her shoes were a delicate shade of lilac.

"Will you come?" Elle asked. "We need your help!"

"Of course we will," said Rachel.

"But how can we leave now? We're surrounded by other children."

Elle smiled.

"Stories make their own magic," she whispered. "The others are too spellbound by the story to notice what's happening."

She waved her wand, and there was a flurry of blue confetti and glittering thimbles. The girls closed their eyes as the magic whirled around, and when they opened them again, they were standing in a vast library. They had been transformed into fairies, and their gossamer wings were fluttering on their backs.

"Welcome to the Fairyland Library," said Elle, giving a delighted twirl.

"It's incredible," Rachel whispered.

"It's the kind of place I've dreamed about," said Kirsty.

The high shelves were a treasure trove of beautiful books with spines in every color of the rainbow. The arched ceiling was made of glass, flooding the room with natural light. Three deep, comfy chairs with plump cushions were

arranged in a horseshoe shape, and three other fairies were curled up on them.

"I'd like to introduce you to the other Storybook Fairies," said Elle, leading Rachel and Kirsty forward. "This is Rosalie the Rapunzel Fairy, Ruth the Red Riding Hood Fairy, and Mariana the Goldilocks Fairy."

Into the Pages

The other fairies jumped up and smiled at Rachel and Kirsty.

"It's wonderful to meet you," Rachel said, recovering from the surprise of being whisked to Fairyland. "But why have you brought us here?"

"I'm afraid that Jack Frost and his goblins have done something truly terrible," said Elle, sinking into one of the chairs.

She raised her wand and pointed it at one of the bookshelves. A large book swept itself off the shelf and opened in midair to a big, blank page. As it hovered there, blurry pictures began to appear on the page. As the

pictures grew clearer, the girls each drew a sharp breath.

"It's a picture of this library," said Kirsty.

"With Jack Frost and his goblins sneaking around inside," Rachel added. "What did they do?"

"They took our most precious belongings," said Elle.

The girls watched the picture in the book. Jack Frost undid the golden clasp of a wooden box. He raised the lid and scooped the contents into a bag, laughing. Then he handed the bag to a goblin, threw the box on the floor, and left the library.

The picture faded, and the book closed itself and slotted back into its place on the shelf.

"What was in the box?" asked Rachel.

"Four magical objects that have power over the stories we protect," said Elle. "Whoever holds the objects has control over the stories. We use them to make sure that the stories go as they are supposed to, so every story ends happily."

"What is Jack Frost using them for?" Kirsty asked.

"He and his goblins are using our magical objects to actually go *into* the stories and change them," said Elle. "They want the stories to be all about them."

Kirsty and Rachel exchanged a worried glance.

"So *that's* why there was a goblin in the Thumbelina story," said Rachel.

"They could spoil the stories forever,"

said Elle,
looking
very upset.
"We have
to do
everything
we can to
stop them,
and that's why
we thought of
you. We know that

you have always been good friends of
Fairyland."

"We will help in any way we can,"
Kirsty promised. "Just tell us what you
would like us to do."

"Help me get my magical thumb ring
back," Elle pleaded. "We'll have to go
into the story and find the goblins."

"Into the story?" Rachel repeated. "Is that possible?"

Elle gave a little smile.

"This is Fairyland," she said. "Anything is possible!"

She flicked her wand, and another book flew from the shelf and into her waiting hands. It had a pale blue cover, and a single word was written on the front in silver letters: *Thumbelina*.

"Come a little closer," said Elle.

Rachel and Kirsty stood on either side of her, and then she waved her wand. In a cloud of rainbow-colored glitter, the girls were swept inside the story of Thumbelina.

Kirsty and Rachel found themselves standing in a cottage. White lace curtains covered the tiny windows, and there was a jug of wild flowers on the wooden kitchen table.

"Oh, we're human again!" Rachel exclaimed.

"Yes," said Elle. "The storybook world is the same size as the human world. Look."

She pointed to a little walnut shell on a nearby windowsill. It was even smaller than she was.

"This must be Thumbelina's bed," Kirsty exclaimed, hurrying over to examine it. "Yes, look, Rachel! There is a tiny pillow and a beautiful quilt made from a rose petal."

Rachel came forward, too, and then paused.

"Do you hear that?" she asked. "It sounds like someone crying."

"Maybe it's Thumbelina!" said Kirsty.

She flung open the window and looked down. Among the bright flowers in the window box was a tiny man wearing a

golden crown. His face was buried in his hands, and he was crying as if his heart were broken.

"It must be the flower fairy prince," said Rachel in a soft voice. "He is supposed to marry Thumbelina at the end of the story."

"That's right," said Elle. "He's a cousin of the Petal Fairies."

The little prince heard them speaking and looked up. He looked horrified when he saw the girls peering down at him.

"Giants!" he cried, jumping to his feet. "Please, don't eat me!"

The Flower Prince

"Don't be scared," said Kirsty. "We're not giants—we're human girls. And we don't want to eat you—we want to help you!"

"No one can help me," groaned the prince, sinking back down into the flowers.

"Why?" asked Elle, flying out the window to hover beside him. "What happened?"

"My dearest love, Thumbelina, has been taken from me by three bright green monsters," said the prince. "They snatched her from her walnut-shell bed and ran off with her."

"Did they have big feet?" Rachel asked.

"And long noses?" Kirsty added.

The prince nodded, and the girls exchanged knowing glances. Goblins!

"I tried to follow them," he said. "I ordered them to bring her back to me. But they just laughed and said that a tiny prince was no match for them, and they were right. There was nothing I could do to get Thumbelina away from them, so I came back here, hoping for a miracle."

"Try not to worry," Rachel said in a soothing voice. "We know exactly who those goblins are, and we've come to help. We'll rescue Thumbelina and we'll get Elle's magical thumb ring back, too."

"Do you know where the goblins took Thumbelina?" Kirsty asked. "Could you take us there?"

The prince looked at the girls with a doubtful expression.

"I only know how to fly there," he said. "I'm not sure I could lead humans on foot."

"That's not a problem for us," said Elle. She waved her wand, and in a whoosh of sparkles, Rachel and Kirsty shrank to fairy size. The prince looked at them in astonishment as they fluttered toward him.

"How marvelous!" he exclaimed.

"Follow me, and I will lead you to where I last saw them."

He zoomed up into the sky on flower-petal wings, and the three fairies followed him. Rachel and Kirsty gazed down at the storybook world as they flew overhead. They passed over a forest and at last reached a wide, burbling stream. There was an island in the middle of the stream, and the prince stopped, hovering in midair.

"There," he said, pointing down to the island. "There they are."

Three goblins were standing around a tree stump in the center of the island. The fairies and the prince flew closer and perched on a low-hanging tree

branch. The goblins did not notice them. They were in the middle of a loud argument.

"I should be the one to wear the magical thumb ring," a short goblin was saying. "After all, I'm the one who captured her. She should marry me!"

He was holding up a silver thumb ring. Then a long-nosed goblin shoved him, knocking the ring onto the tree stump.

"No way!" the long-nosed goblin said, grabbing the ring. "It fits my hand much better than yours."

"I'm the oldest, so the ring should be mine!" shrieked a knobby-kneed goblin, snatching the ring and kissing it.

"She doesn't want to marry any of them," said the flower prince. "I am hoping that she wants to marry me! But where is she?"

They looked around, and then the prince drew in a sharp breath and grabbed Kirsty's arm.

"There she is," he said. "Look—on the tree stump."

The fairies looked and saw a tiny girl, no bigger than a human thumb, running back and forth across the tree stump. She was trying to grab the ring that the goblins were throwing around, but she was much too small.

"Come on, let's go help her!" the prince exclaimed.

"Wait," said Rachel, putting her hand on his arm. "We have to get Elle's thumb ring back, too, or you and Thumbelina won't get your happily ever after ending."

"But we can't leave her there with those goblins!" the prince cried.

"We need to distract them," said Kirsty, thinking hard. "Could you swoop down toward them and try to keep them talking to you? Maybe we can get the thumb ring while they're not looking."

The prince nodded.

"I love Thumbelina!" he declared, throwing his tiny hands in the air. "I will do whatever it takes to rescue her from the goblins!"

Brave Thumbelina

The flower prince swooped down
toward the goblins, shouting as he flew.

"Let Thumbelina go!" he demanded.
"You don't belong in our story!"

The goblins jumped up and darted
toward him, raising their hands and
trying to swat him like a fly.

"Hooray!" Thumbelina shouted, delighted to see the prince. "Now you goblins will be sorry!"

"No pint-sized prince is going to stop us!" the short goblin shrieked.

Meanwhile, the three fairies zoomed down toward the goblin with the thumb ring. He wasn't paying attention to the ring—it would be easy to slip it off his thumb without him noticing. But just as Kirsty was about to grab it, the long-nosed goblin took it. He shoved it onto his thumb and folded his fingers over it.

"Hey, that's mine!" the knobby-kneed goblin wailed. "Give it back!"

The goblins splashed into the shallow stream, shouting and squabbling. They pushed and shoved, dunking one another under the water and spluttering with fury. But the whole time, the long-nosed goblin kept dancing around in front of them.

"I'm going to live happily ever after!" he taunted in a singsong voice. "You two might as well go marry toads!"

Snickering and gloating, he danced farther out into the stream. Meanwhile, the prince flew over to the tree stump and put his arms around Thumbelina.

"I will find a way to save you from these goblins," he promised.

"But how?" asked Thumbelina. "They're so much bigger than us."

"Size doesn't matter," said Rachel, smiling at the girl. "You've got fairies and magic and friendship on your side. I know that we can stop those goblins. We just have to think of a good plan to get the thumb ring back, and then everything will be all right."

"I don't think anything will make the goblins give up the ring," said Thumbelina. "I've been listening to them, and it's all they talk about."

"I have an idea!" Rachel exclaimed. "Rings are really important in fairy tale weddings. We can offer a trade. Elle, could you magically create another ring?"

Elle waved her wand, and there was a faint magical tinkle as a sparkly green ring dropped onto the tree stump beside them. It glimmered in the sunshine and immediately caught the eye of the long-nosed goblin. He splashed out of the stream and hurried over to it, his arm outstretched.

"Mine!" he squawked.

Kirsty seized the ring and flew upward, holding it out of his reach.

"If you want this, you have to return Elle's thumb ring first," she said.

"Give it!" hollered the goblin, jumping up and down and trying to reach Kirsty. "I want it now!"

Rachel fluttered up and hovered in front of the goblin.

"You're not thinking clearly," she said. "If you're going to have a fairy tale wedding, you have to exchange rings with Thumbelina. If Thumbelina gives you the green ring, surely you could give her the thumb ring."

The goblin thought about this for

a moment, but he still didn't seem convinced.

"If I were lucky enough to marry Thumbelina, I would certainly give her a ring," said the flower prince.

"Fine," snapped the goblin. "I'll give Thumbelina the ring on one condition. We have the fairy tale wedding I've always wanted right now!"

"I'll do it," Thumbelina said.

Thumbelina winked at Rachel and Kirsty.

"This goblin really wants a fairy tale wedding!" she whispered. "Once he hands me the ring, you can swoop in and grab it."

Rachel and Kirsty nodded.

"Once I have my ring back, your story will go back to normal," Elle promised.

Woodland Wedding

Thumbelina and the fairies stood on the tree stump, watching as the goblin smoothed down his bumpy head and put a moth-eaten green tie around his neck.

"What do you think? Is this fancy enough?" he asked Thumbelina.

"Sure, you look great," Thumbelina said, stifling a giggle behind her hand.

Rachel and Kirsty rolled their eyes.

"I don't care," said the goblin. "I just can't wait to see the faces of the other goblins in Goblin Grotto when they hear about this!"

He rubbed his hands together and the flower prince groaned. He couldn't believe the goblin could be so easily tricked. But then, he hadn't met many goblins!

The other two goblins were looking very grumpy. They had found some old vests for the occasion, but they were a pretty tight fit.

"I will conduct the ceremony," said Elle, stepping onto the highest point of the tree stump.

Thumbelina stood in front of her, and

the goblin knelt down beside the tree stump.

"First, you must exchange your rings," said Elle. "Goblin, give Thumbelina her ring."

"Give me my ring first," demanded the goblin.

Elle shook her head.

"You first," she said. "That's how it should be done."

Grumbling, the goblin took the thumb ring off and placed it in front of Thumbelina. It was much too big for her to wear, but she pushed it toward Elle.

As soon as the little fairy touched the ring, it shrank to the right size. Elle slipped it onto her thumb and smiled.

"Hey, that ring's for Thumbelina!" the goblin protested. "Give it back!"

Kirsty handed the sparkly green ring to Thumbelina, who held it out to the goblin.

"This is for you to keep," she said. "But you're not getting a fairy tale wedding today. I want to marry the flower prince!"

With that, she ran into the prince's arms and the two of them embraced joyfully. Suddenly, bells started to

chime all around them. Rachel clapped
her hands in delight.

"They're bluebells!" she cried.

"They're telling all the woodland
creatures that there will be a wedding
today," said Elle.

She waved her wand, and
Thumbelina's dress
transformed into
a wedding
gown made
of white
rose petals.
She wore
a cobweb
veil, held
in place by
a golden
tiara.

From all around, woodland animals splashed across the stream to join them on the little island. Soon there was a huge congregation of wedding guests, and nightingales perched in the trees and sang for the happy couple.

Elle led the ceremony, and Rachel and Kirsty were bridesmaids. The prince and Thumbelina gave each other sparkling dewdrop rings.

"I now declare you husband and wife!" said Elle.

"Hooray!" cried Rachel and Kirsty. "Three cheers for Thumbelina!"

The bluebells started to chime again, and the woodland guests erupted in cheers and applause. Even the goblins celebrated, throwing handfuls of flower petal confetti at Thumbelina and her prince. Tears rolled down the cheeks of the long-nosed goblin,

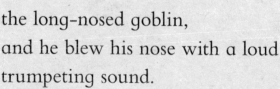

and he blew his nose with a loud trumpeting sound.

"I love weddings!" he sniffed.

After the ceremony, there was dancing and a magnificent feast. Rachel and Kirsty wished that their storybook adventure could go on forever, but after a while, Elle fluttered over and put her arms around them.

"It's time to go," she whispered. "Thank you for helping me fix my story."

"Thank you for bringing us here," Kirsty replied.

Elle raised her wand, and the beautiful woodland scene disappeared in a whoosh of fairy dust. When the sparkles faded, the girls found themselves sitting beside the river at the Storytelling Festival. As usual, no time had passed since they left. The children were still sitting around the book bench, and Alana Yarn was still reading *Thumbelina* aloud.

"The toad lived in a swampy stream in the garden," she said. "He croaked when he saw Thumbelina."

Rachel and Kirsty exchanged smiles of relief and happiness. The story was back to normal. They settled back to enjoy listening. When Alana came to the part about Thumbelina and the flower prince getting married, they felt a thrill of excitement.

"All their woodland friends came to the wedding, and their fairy friends, too," Alana read.

"I can't believe it!" said Rachel in a whisper. "We're in the story!"

"It was a wonderful wedding," said Kirsty. "I'll never forget it."

The best friends smiled at each other, but then Kirsty looked thoughtful.

"I wonder which story Jack Frost and the goblins will want to change next," she said. "I hope that we can get the rest of the magical objects back for the other Storybook Fairies."

Rachel thought of the beautiful woodland wedding they had just seen and the magic that Elle had performed. Then she looked around at the rapt faces of the other children.

"We will," she said, feeling determined. "Stories are too important to let Jack Frost ruin them!"

RAINBOW
magic™
THE STORYBOOK FAIRIES

Rachel and Kirsty found Elle's
missing magic thumb ring. Now it's
time for them to help

Mariana
the Goldilocks Fairy!

Join their next adventure in
this special sneak peek ...

Puppet Problems

Kirsty Tate was walking along the river path toward the Story Barge, feeling thrilled to her fingertips. She loved books, and the Wetherbury Storytelling Festival was like a dream come true for her. Even better, she was enjoying every moment with her best friend, Rachel Walker, who was staying for the whole weekend.

"This day just gets better and better," said Rachel, grabbing Kirsty's hand. "The Storybook Picnic was amazing, and now we're going to see a puppet show put on by Alana Yarn. I can't wait!"

Alana Yarn was one of their favorite authors. She was running the festival, which was being held in Wetherbury Park. The girls were attending every event they could. They had just come from a giant picnic, where they had eaten food inspired by their favorite stories. There had even been a cake in the shape of a very large storybook.

"What was your favorite food at the picnic?" Kirsty asked as they reached the Story Barge.

"I can't decide," said Rachel after a

moment's pause. "I loved the *Alice in Wonderland* EAT ME cupcakes, but the *Peter Pan* cake pops were delicious, too."

They were standing next to the Story Barge now, and there was a sign on the path advertising the show.

ALANA YARN'S PUPPET SHOW

COME INSIDE AND GUESS THE STORY

"Come on!" said Kirsty.

She stepped onto the creaky old Story Barge. A short ladder led to the upper deck, which was piled with books. Inviting armchairs and plump floor cushions were scattered around. Lots of children were already on board, looking very excited.

"Let's find a seat," said Rachel. "I want to look at all these books."

The girls settled down on a large blue

cushion, and they were soon sharing a book that they had been longing to read. Just as they finished the first chapter and exchanged happy smiles, a head popped up from the wooden staircase that led down to the lower deck of the barge. It was Alana Yarn.

"The puppet show is ready," she announced. "Come on down to the lower deck, everyone. A story is waiting for you!"

The children made their way downstairs and gathered on large pillows in the middle of the lower deck. At the far end of the deck, Rachel and Kirsty saw a small stage with a tall striped puppet theater and a large trunk. The trunk had a curved lid, decorated with pictures of fairy tale characters. Alana was standing in front of the trunk, and as soon as all the children were sitting down, she lifted the lid.

"I'd like you to try to guess what story I'm going to tell," she told the listening children. "Look carefully at the puppets and see if you can figure it out."

First, she took out a large hand puppet of a girl with long blond hair. Then she placed some props on the stage.

RAINBOW magic™

Which Magical Fairies Have You Met?

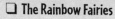

- ☐ The Rainbow Fairies
- ☐ The Weather Fairies
- ☐ The Jewel Fairies
- ☐ The Pet Fairies
- ☐ The Sports Fairies
- ☐ The Ocean Fairies
- ☐ The Princess Fairies
- ☐ The Superstar Fairies
- ☐ The Fashion Fairies
- ☐ The Sugar & Spice Fairies
- ☐ The Earth Fairies
- ☐ The Magical Crafts Fairies
- ☐ The Baby Animal Rescue Fairies
- ☐ The Fairy Tale Fairies
- ☐ The School Day Fairies

▮▮ SCHOLASTIC

Find all of your favorite fairy friends at
scholastic.com/rainbowmagic

HiT entertainment

RMFAIRY15

SPECIAL EDITION

Which Magical Fairies Have You Met?

- ❏ Joy the Summer Vacation Fairy
- ❏ Holly the Christmas Fairy
- ❏ Kylie the Carnival Fairy
- ❏ Stella the Star Fairy
- ❏ Shannon the Ocean Fairy
- ❏ Trixie the Halloween Fairy
- ❏ Gabriella the Snow Kingdom Fairy
- ❏ Juliet the Valentine Fairy
- ❏ Mia the Bridesmaid Fairy
- ❏ Flora the Dress-Up Fairy
- ❏ Paige the Christmas Play Fairy
- ❏ Emma the Easter Fairy
- ❏ Cara the Camp Fairy
- ❏ Destiny the Rock Star Fairy
- ❏ Belle the Birthday Fairy
- ❏ Olympia the Games Fairy

- ❏ Selena the Sleepover Fairy
- ❏ Cheryl the Christmas Tree Fairy
- ❏ Florence the Friendship Fairy
- ❏ Lindsay the Luck Fairy
- ❏ Brianna the Tooth Fairy
- ❏ Autumn the Falling Leaves Fairy
- ❏ Keira the Movie Star Fairy
- ❏ Addison the April Fool's Day Fairy
- ❏ Bailey the Babysitter Fairy
- ❏ Natalie the Christmas Stocking Fairy
- ❏ Lila and Myla the Twins Fairies
- ❏ Chelsea the Congratulations Fairy
- ❏ Carly the School Fairy
- ❏ Angelica the Angel Fairy
- ❏ Blossom the Flower Girl Fairy
- ❏ Skyler the Fireworks Fairy
- ❏ Giselle the Christmas Ballet Fairy

■ SCHOLASTIC

Find all of your favorite fairy friends at
scholastic.com/rainbowmagic

3 stories in each one!

HIT entertainment

RMSPECIAL19

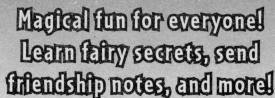

RAINBOW magic™

Magical fun for everyone!
Learn fairy secrets, send
friendship notes, and more!

■SCHOLASTIC

HiT entertainment

www.scholastic.com/rainbowmagic

RMACTIV4